# The Three Wishes

## JOANNA HARRISON

Collins

*An imprint of* HarperCollins*Publishers*

*For my father*

*Other titles by Joanna Harrison:*
When Mum Turned Into A Monster
Dear Bear

First published in hardback in Great Britain by
HarperCollins Publishers Ltd in 1999.
First published in Picture Lions in 2000.

1 3 5 7 9 10 8 6 4 2

ISBN: 0 00 6646441

Picture Lions is an imprint of the Children's Division,
part of HarperCollins Publishers Ltd.

Text and illustrations copyright © Joanna Harrison 1999.

The author/illustrator asserts the moral right to be
identified as the author/illustrator of the work.

A CIP catalogue record for this title is
available from the British Library.

Printed in Hong Kong.

Lulu was making a fairy costume. She'd taken some old wings from the dressing-up box, cut out a star, stuck it on a stick to make a wand and found some beautiful, glittery material that would be perfect for a dress.

But the dress needed sewing and Lulu didn't know how.

"Can you help me?" she asked her mum.
"Not now, Lulu," said her mum.
"I'm busy. Maybe later."

"How about now?" said Lulu.
"Later!" said Mum.

"Now?" said Lulu hopefully.
"It's too late," said Mum. "Time you were in bed!"

Later that night, Lulu was woken by a scratching sound.

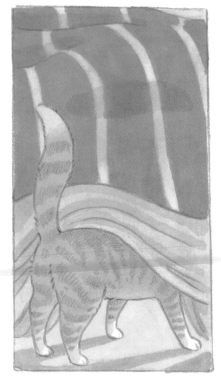

It was the cat trying to get at something under the bed!

"I hope it's not another mouse," thought Lulu. She picked up the cat and put him outside the door.

She jumped back on to her bed and peered underneath.

It wasn't a mouse at all…

...it was a fairy!

"Thank you for rescuing me," she said, coming out from under the bed.
"Oh, it was n..n..nothing," stammered Lulu.

"Even so," replied the fairy, "I'd like to give you a special present... one that only fairies can give."

"What's that?" asked Lulu.
"THREE WISHES," said the fairy.

"Three wishes!" said Lulu. "Does that mean I can wish for anything I like?"

"Anything!" replied the fairy.
So Lulu thought and thought.

She thought of her fairy dress and how much she would like it made properly, and her wand that needed mending…

And then she had a better idea.

"I *WISH* I were a fairy," said Lulu.

"A *real* fairy."

All of a sudden, Lulu found she had shrunk to a very small size...

and on her back was a pair of beautiful wings.

She tried flapping them...

but nothing happened.

So she tried again and again...

until, suddenly, she found herself *flying*...

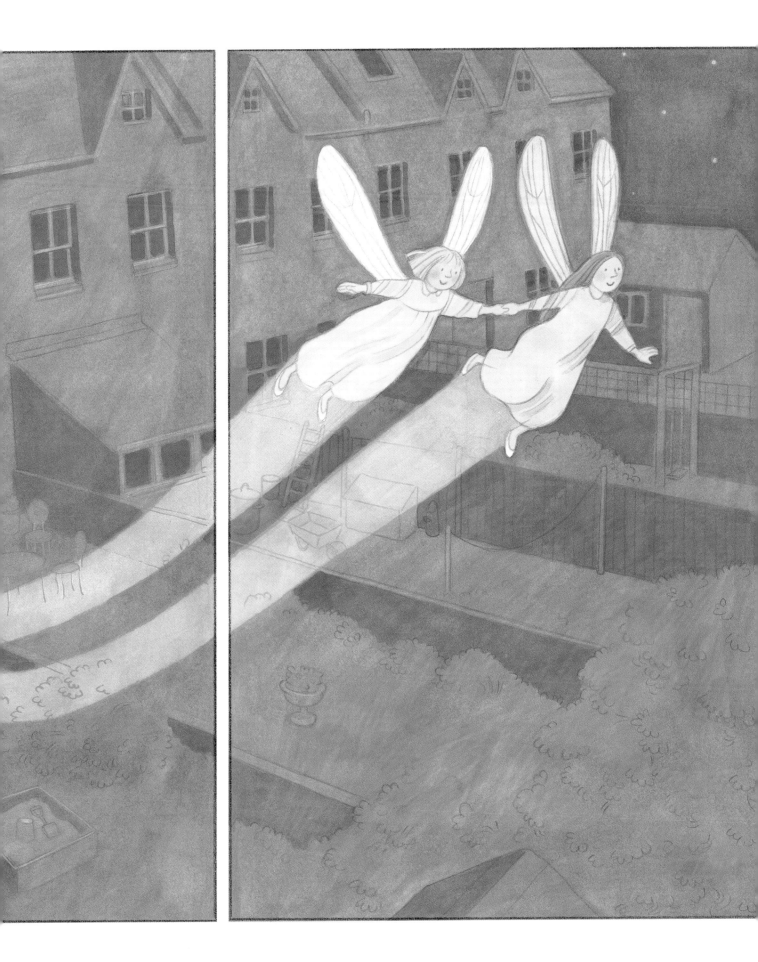

"Follow me," called the fairy, and they circled and swooped over the back garden.

They danced on the TV aerial,

and fluttered with the moths around the light.

They peered in through Mum and Dad's bedroom window,

and made sand castles in the sandpit, and splashed in the
paddling pool.

Then they tried to play on the climbing frame, but nearly got stuck in a spider's web!

And as they munched through leftover crisps, and drank
what they could from a carton of juice…

they didn't notice the cat

creeping up behind them,

waiting to...

**POUNCE!**

"Back to my bedroom," shouted Lulu.
"We'll be safe there."

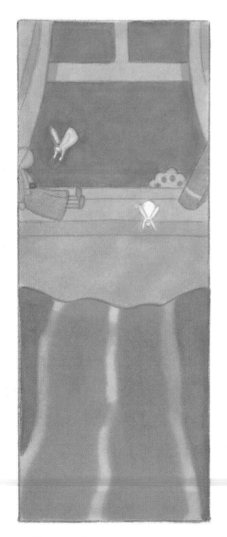  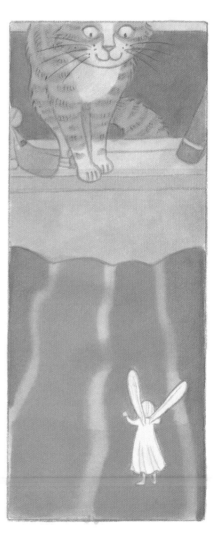

But the cat jumped on to the windowsill. Lulu panicked.
"I *WISH* I weren't a fairy any more!" she cried.

And, suddenly, it was morning and Lulu was sitting on her bed, with the cat on her lap.

The door opened. It was Mum.

"Lulu, are you okay? You look as
if you've been up all night."
"But I *have!*" said Lulu.

"I've been flying around the back garden and I even danced on the roof."

"What an extraordinary dream," said Mum.

"But it wasn't a dream!" cried Lulu. "Look at my wings!"

"What wings?" asked Mum.

"Oh, they've gone," said Lulu. "But I *did* have wings. Ask the fairy."

"What fairy?" said Mum.

Lulu looked everywhere but the fairy was nowhere to be seen.

"Maybe it *was* just a dream," said Lulu sadly.

"I don't think I want to be a fairy anyway," said Lulu at breakfast. "It's fun, but it's too dangerous. Did I tell you how I dreamed I nearly got stuck in a spider's web? That was scary!

And then… Mum… are you listening to me?

Oh, I *WISH* you weren't always so busy!"

And, suddenly, Mum just stopped washing up.

"Busy!" exclaimed Mum. "Me? Busy? Never!"

So what did Mum do? She dried her hands, left the washing-up and took a large tin of biscuits down from the shelf.

As they sat round the kitchen table, Lulu told her mum all about the beautiful fairy in her dream.

"I tell you what," said her mum. "Why don't I finish making your fairy dress for you?"

So she stuck the star back on the wand,

straightened the wings

and sewed the beautiful, glittery material into a fairy dress for Lulu.

Lulu put the dress on.

"You look just like a real fairy," said Mum.

"I *WISH* I were a real fairy…" said Lulu, "just like in my dream."

But, by now, Lulu had used up all her three wishes…
and that was probably just as well.